Muriel
and the
Monster Maniac
Spell

Muriel
and the Monster Maniac Spell

Angie Sage

Hodder
Children's
Books

a division of Hodder Headline plc

For the two Pookies with love

First published in Great Britain in 1995
by Hodder Children's Books

The right of Angie Sage to be identified as the Author and Illustrator of the Work has been asserted by her in accordance with the Copyright, Designs and Patents Act 1988.

10 9 8 7 6 5 4 3 2 1

A Catalogue record for this book is available from the British Library

ISBN 0340 64845 7

Printed and bound in Great Britain by
Cox & Wyman Ltd, Reading, Berks.

Hodder Children's Books
A Division of Hodder Headline plc
338 Euston Road
London NW1 3BH

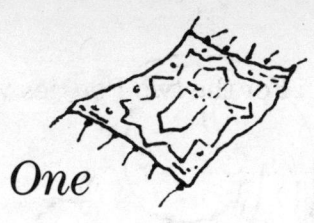

One

Theobald was a quiet elephant who liked nothing better than to sit on his cushion and read his book, *Fun With Simple Spells*. But he had never managed to sit on his cushion and read for longer than four minutes and twenty-three seconds. Theobald knew this because he had a stop-watch and he knew the reason why, too. The reason was Muriel, Student Magician Grade One (repeat year).

So, one sunny morning, when Theobald's stop-watch was ticking round to three minutes and fifty-two seconds, he was not suprised when he heard, 'Theobald! Come *on* !'

Muriel rushed into the room and grabbed Theobald off the cushion. She lifted him up, shoved him under her arm and ran up the steps to the castle roof.

You may be wondering if Student Magician Muriel was extremely strong but, in fact, it was Theobald who was extremely small – for an elephant. Theobald was an unusual sort of elephant. Muriel's Aunt

Emilene had made him for Muriel as a helper and spellmaker. Muriel lived with her Aunt Emilene in the west wing of Crumbled Castle and Aunt Emilene knew a lot of strange things.

Theobald was, in fact, made out of a large pair of socks and stuffed with Aunt Emilene's tights, but Muriel was usually careful not to mention that unless Theobald had made her really cross.

When Muriel and Theobald arrived on the castle roof, Muriel gave a loud, piercing whistle. She looked up into the sky and tapped her foot impatiently.

'Mu . . .' puffed Theobald, who had just got his breath back, 'did the Magician say you could go out?'

Muriel did not answer.

'Mu,' said Theobald crossly, 'you'll *never* get through your Grade One if you keep bunking off.'

'It's crazy up in that tower, Theo,' said

Muriel, 'You wouldn't believe it, he's gone bonkers at last–'

Theobald was shocked. 'Muriel, that's no way to talk about a member of the Magicians' Moot.'

'But Theo, he's got stuff flying all over the place. I think he's messed up a spell, he's running around like a headless chicken.'

'Mu, he's a qualified magician, he wouldn't mess up a spell. You should have more respect,' Theobald tut-tutted.

'Well, Auntie Ems says that ever since Boris disappeared he's been hopeless with spells. Anyway, he didn't even *look* at my thunderflash project. Instead, I ended up sorting out his smelly old socks and ironing his hat. I was there for hours.'

'Three minutes and fifty-two seconds, actually Mu.'

Muriel shuffled her feet and looked up at the sky again. 'Here's one, Theo!' she said. Muriel grabbed hold of Theobald's arm and dragged him over to a small scruffy carpet that was wafting down from the sky on to the castle roof.

Muriel pushed Theobald on to the carpet as it hovered quietly. Theobald held his trunk. 'Smells mouldy, Mu. Can't we wait for another one?'

The carpet shook itself crossly and clouds of dust flew around Muriel and Theobald.

'Aaah . . . aaahh . . .' Theobald began to sneeze and Muriel put one hand over his mouth and tightly held on to his trunk with the other one.

'Where to?' asked the carpet in a bored voice.

'Somewhere else,' said Muriel. 'Anywhere but here will be just fine, thank you.'

'. . . TCHOO!'

'OUCH!' Theobald had accidently-on-purpose bitten Muriel's thumb.

The carpet took off with Muriel and Theobald hanging on to its dusty edges. As it flew up past the Magician's tower Muriel tried to look as if she wasn't there.

The Magician stuck his head out of the window. 'STOP!' he boomed.

'Bother!' said Muriel under her breath as the carpet stopped for the Magician, as all carpets are trained to do.

'You forgot your homework,' said the Magician. He gave Muriel a sheet of paper covered with strange signs and symbols. 'This is for your project on spellmakers. It's about my dear departed Boris Borrible, the very best spellmaker and helper a magician could ever hope for, *sniff*. I want you to know it backwards and sideways by midnight tonight and – oh bother!' The Magician waved his arms around as though he was swatting some rather nasty wasps and shouted at something in the tower, 'Stop it! LET GO!' Then he disappeared from the window.

He reappeared clutching another piece of paper. 'Get me these from the Magic Shop, Muriel,' he puffed in a flustered voice as he gave her a shopping list. 'These are *very* important and I must have them as soon as possible. It's the only way to stop this – OH, GET OFF ME!' The Magician pushed something away from him and then turned to Muriel and Theobald.

'GO!' yelled the Magician, and the carpet shot off at top speed, completely forgetting about Muriel and Theobald who very nearly fell off as it steeply climbed up and over the castle.

'Bother, bother, bother!' muttered Muriel when she got her breath back. 'I thought he had forgotten my homework.' She noticed Theobald's expression. 'There's no need to look so smug,' she hissed.

'It's about time you did some homework,' snorted Theobald. 'I wonder what he had in the tower? I hope he's all right.'

'Of course he's all right,' snapped Muriel, 'I told you he was going bonkers, didn't I?' Theobald was about to say something when Muriel grumpily stuck her tongue out at him.

'Huh!' muttered Theobald crossly.

The carpet flew high over the mountains, swooping and diving in the air currents, and curved gracefully down to the village where the Magic Shop was.

Muriel and Theobald sat at opposite ends, not speaking to each other.

 *Two*

They landed with a bump outside the Magic Shop. The carpet shook itself and Muriel and Theobald fell off.

'Mouldy indeed!' muttered the carpet as it flew off in a cloud of dust.

A strange purple light flickered round the front of the Magic Shop.

Muriel stood and looked at the spiky green door which was tightly shut. She had only been there once before with the Magician and the only thing she knew for sure was that you had to wait to be asked in.

Muriel wondered if anyone knew she was outside. Then she wondered if anyone would ask her in; suppose they kept her waiting there all day? Just then the door glowed and said in a squeaky voice, 'Welcome Muriel, student of Godfrey,

14

Magician of the Crumbled Castle. Welcome
Theobald, Elephant Spellmaker of Muriel.
Step this way please.'

The door dissolved into a pool of green light and Muriel and Theobald walked in, very carefully, because they were not at all sure what to expect next. Theobald slipped his paw into Muriel's hand and Muriel gave it a grateful squeeze as they stood together in the middle of a long hazy hall that seemed to go on forever.

Bright signs advertising things like Piranha Potions and Gerbil Jellies blinked on and off and ghostly lights swirled round them. There were small tinkly sounds like bells ringing and a deeper rumbling sound that seemed to come from underneath their feet.

It was not a very comfortable place to be in.

Soon they heard another sound, a distant clanking coming towards them. Muriel peered through the green mist that hung round them and saw . . . a shopping trolley.

The trolley rattled up towards them, skidding sideways as shopping trolleys do, and came to a halt on Theobald's left foot.

'OW!' yelled Theobald.

A small and rather digusting Spotty Something was sitting in the child seat of the trolley. It stuck its head out and breathed over Muriel.

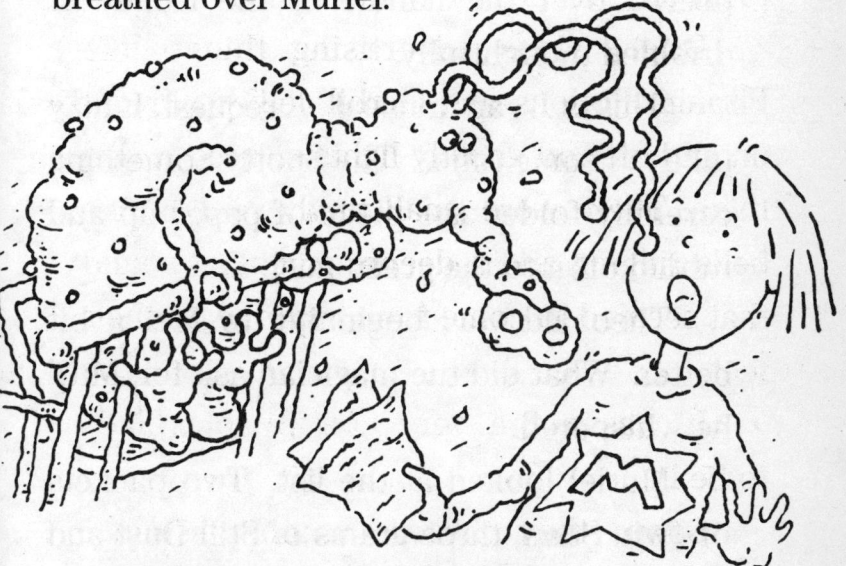

Muriel screamed, 'AAAGH!'

'May I have . . . your order . . . please?' hissed the Spotty Something as it waved its antennae in Muriel's face.

Muriel quickly shoved a piece of paper into one of its feelers and sat down on the floor next to Theobald who was already sitting down holding his foot. She felt a little shaky.

The Spotty Something looked at the piece of paper for a long time and then peered over the handle of the trolley. It dribbled thoughtfully.

'This is . . . an unusual . . . request. It may take . . . some time.' The Spotty Something carefully folded the piece of paper up and rattled off into the green mist.

Theobald was beginning to feel a bit better. 'What did the magician ask for, Mu?' he whispered.

Muriel looked at the list. 'Two packets of Twin Stars, three grams of Still Dust and a tube of Truth Paste,' she read.

'Oh,' said Theobald thoughtfully. Then he said, 'Mu, how come you've still got the list?'

Muriel stared at the list in her hand. She looked puzzled.

'Mu,' whispered Theobald, 'you gave that . . . thing . . . your homework instead of the shopping list.'

'AAAGH!' Muriel screamed for the second time and held her hands over her mouth in horror. Theobald thought that Muriel was getting very jumpy.

The shopping trolley containing the Spotty Something and a large blue box trundled out of the mist. The large blue box had bright red signs all over it, they said things like 'DO NOT DISTURB', 'KEEP CLEAR WHEN ADDING WATER' and 'THIS WAY UP'.

The Spotty Something looked at Muriel closely. 'Tell Magician Godfrey . . . that we did not know . . . that we had this. However . . . we are not responsible for–'

'Yes, but look I've made a mistake!' said Muriel, waving the magician's shopping list at the Spotty Something.

'It is *our* mistake . . . please apologise
. . . there will be no charge.'

'But, but–' stammered Muriel.

The Spotty Something ignored her and
shoved the box into her hands. 'Please take
. . . it is late . . . we are closing now.'

At that the Spotty Something began
pushing Muriel and Theobald towards the
door. 'We are closing . . . please leave now.
Goodbye goodbye goodbye . . . Thank you
thank you thank you.'

Suddenly Muriel and Theobald were
standing outside the Magic Shop holding the
blue box. It was beginning to get dark. 'We
were only in there for a few minutes,' said
Muriel. 'What's happened to the rest of
the day?'

'We were in there for nine hours, five
minutes and thirty-seven seconds,'
announced Theobald as he shook his stop-
watch. 'Time warp, Mu. You do that in Grade

Two. *If* you ever get to Grade Two of course, which you won't if you keep giving your homework away!'

'Oh, stop being such a goody-goody Theo. Let's just get home, shall we?' snapped Muriel. She whistled for a carpet. The sound echoed round the houses.

'There's no point doing that, Mu,' sniffed Theobald as he stood on the deserted pavement next to a blue box and a grumpy Muriel. 'Carpets don't fly in the dark.'

'WHAT? No one ever told me that!' exclaimed a shocked Muriel. 'What are we going to do now?'

Three

Muriel and Theobald looked along the dark empty street. All the houses had their doors locked and barred and their curtains tightly closed. It was very quiet except for the hissing of the gas-lamp that they were standing under.

'Bother!' said Muriel. 'What a really horrible, horrible day. We're stuck here in this nasty, spooky dump and the Magician will be cross because we're late and I haven't done my homework and we haven't got his shopping and all we've got is this *stupid* box –' Muriel gave the box a kick '– and it's dark and creepy and . . .' Muriel sniffed and tried to find her hanky.

A few drops of water began to land on

Theobald's trunk. 'Don't cry, Mu, it will be all right,' said Theobald, although he was not at all sure if it would be.

'I'm not crying,' said Muriel crossly.

CRACKLE . . . CRASH! A flash of lightning leapt across the sky. There was a clap of thunder and rain began to pour down.

'I don't believe this,' muttered Muriel as the rain ran down the back of her neck and sploshed into her shoes. It whooshed and drummed on the blue box which was now sitting in a puddle on the pavement. The box was getting very soggy and steam began to seep out of the top of it.

'Look, Theo!' yelled Muriel, pointing up the dark street. Theobald looked. There were two bright lights coming towards them. There was a muffled roaring noise and a loud rattling banging mixed in with a teeth-on-edge grinding sound as the lights drew nearer.

'It's a bus, it's a bus, it's a BUS!' yelled Muriel. She jumped up and down excitedly and waved her arms to stop the bus. There was a terrible screeching and smell of

burning rubber as the bus shuddered to a halt.

'But we don't know where it's going,' protested Theobald.

'Who cares,' said Muriel. 'Anywhere's better than this creepy place.' She picked up the squelchy blue box in one arm and Theobald in the other and got on to the bus.

Muriel did not rush upstairs and sit at the front as usual, she was too tired and wet. She dumped Theobald and the soggy blue box on to one of the nearest seats and sat down thankfully next to them.

The bus conductor slithered towards them. She was slimy and strange, but not nearly as bad as the Spotty Something.

'Two halves to wherever you're going, please,' said Muriel politely. The conductor gave Muriel two tickets and slid off to her little seat under the stairs.

'Where's the bus going to then, Mu?' asked Theobald.

'Doesn't matter.' said Muriel tiredly. 'At least it's dry in here.'

Theobald and Muriel sat quietly in the bumpy old bus as it rattled along the road and lurched round corners. They tried to look out of the window to see where they were going but it was far too dark. The rain streamed down outside the window and every now and then they could hear thunder. The wind blew against the bus and made it sway from side to side.

The bumpy ride and the warm bus began to make Muriel sleepy, but as she began to doze off she heard a scrabbling sound.

'Shut up, Theo,' she said sleepily.

Theobald poked her in the ribs. Muriel sat up crossly,

'Mu . . .' whispered Theobald in a worried voice, 'what's that noise?'

It was coming from the blue box. Muriel looked at it and gasped, 'Theo, what's happening?' The blue box was beginning to come apart at the seams. There was something inside it, something that seemed

to be moving. Something that was making little scrabbling noises.

'Oh crumbs . . .' muttered Muriel. 'What is it?'

Theobald peeled off a wet piece of paper that was stuck to the side of the box. The piece of paper said:

CONGRATULATIONS

You are now the proud owner of a ~ Borrible ~

a MUST for any Modern Magician

This box contains one DRIED 500gm Borrible and is sold by weight, not volume.

INSTRUCTIONS

Add water and stand well back

DO NOT USE IN A CONFINED SPACE

'What's a confined space, Theo?' asked Muriel.

'Somewhere sort of small inside, Mu,' said Theobald.

'Like a bus, you mean?'

'Yes, like a bus. MU! GET IT OFF THE BUS!' Theobald jumped down from the seat. 'Quick Mu, throw it out of the door before it gets too big, before it squashes us all flat!'

Muriel picked up the Borrible box, which was beginning to sizzle, and started to run towards the door of the bus. Then she realised that the box was now very very hot: 'Ouch!' Muriel dropped the Borrible box.

The bus was going up a steep hill; the box skidded along the floor, taking Theobald with it, and crashed into the back of the bus. The box fell to pieces and a small squashy Borrible landed on top of Theobald.

Theobald scrambled out from underneath the Borrible. The Borrible sat up and licked Theobald's ear.

'Oh, isn't it sweet, Mu?' cooed Theobald, who had quite forgotten about getting the Borrible off the bus.

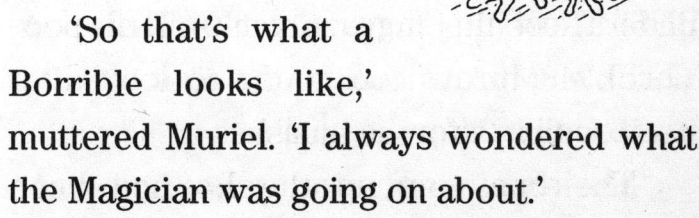

'So that's what a Borrible looks like,' muttered Muriel. 'I always wondered what the Magician was going on about.'

As the bus ploughed through a deep puddle, a spray of water came in through the door and landed on the Borrible. Suddenly it started to grow – *fast*. It was as though someone was blowing up a huge blue balloon. The Borrible grew and grew until it was squashing Muriel and Theobald up against the inside of the bus.

'Mnnfff!' grunted Theobald as he disappeared underneath the luggage rack. Muriel was stuck in a small corner by the stairs.

'Can't breathe . . .' she puffed. 'Get OFF!' She gave the Borrible a huge push, it popped out of the door like a cork out of a bottle and disappeared into the night with a loud squeak.

Theobald struggled out from underneath the luggage rack. 'That poor Borrible, Mu, it's too young to look after itself. Quick, stop the bus!'

The bus conductor, who had been woken up by Muriel treading on her, rang the bell. The bus stopped but Muriel did not want to get off. 'Look Theo, let's not go out in that storm, we can come back for the Borrible later . . .'

Theobald ignored her. He jumped off the bus and ran back along the road towards the Borrible.

'Troublemakers!' muttered the bus conductor. She pushed Muriel off the bus and crossly rang the bell. The bus roared off into the night.

Muriel found herself standing alone on a dark and empty road. She shivered, the rain dripped off the end of her nose and the wind howled round her. Muriel began to feel scared.

Four

Meanwhile, back at Crumbled Castle, the Magician was in his tower trying to dodge out of the way of a very nasty spell which was swirling round him in a smelly black cloud.

It was already dark, the rain was pouring down and the wind was howling through the castle. The Magician was worried; there was no sign of Muriel and the shopping. The Magician needed the shopping very badly. It was the only way that he knew how to stop the spell. He had to shake two packets of Twin Stars over it, blow three grams of Still Dust at it and then squirt it with a tube of Truth Paste. Of course, the Magician should have had Twin Stars, Still Dust and Truth Paste in his store cupboard, but ever since Boris Borrible had mysteriously disappeared one dark night he had not bothered much with store cupboards.

The Magician looked at his sticky spellbook which lay open in front of him.

Like all Magicians, he had his very own spellbook; it was a huge, magic scrapbook, full of spells which he had collected together over the years. He sighed. To think that he, Godfrey, Magician of Crumbled Castle, member of the Magicians' Moot and recently voted 'The Magician your mum would most like to meet', had messed up a spell.

'It would never have happened if Boris had still been here,' he muttered miserably.

It had all started two days earlier when he had looked up a special Happy Birthday Spell for his sister, Aunt Emilene. He was halfway through the spell – and a rather tasty jam sandwich which Muriel had left in her lunch box – when a washbasin dived out of a window on the other side of the castle and landed in the moat. Aunt Emilene was feeding the ducks at the time and it only just missed her.

This kind of thing kept happening at Crumbled Castle. Only the week before, a sack of manure had mysteriously jumped off a parapet and landed all over the Magician while he was weeding the cabbage patch.

When he had come back from pulling Aunt Emilene out of the moat and setting one of the duck's legs in plaster, the Magician started the spell again. Unfortunately he did not notice that Muriel's jam sandwich had somehow got squashed in the spellbook and two of the pages were stuck together. He turned over the pages and carried on with a Monster Maniac Spell.

Soon, the Happy Birthday Spell was well and truly mixed up with the worst ever

Monster Maniac Spell.

At first, the Happy Birthday Monster Maniac Spell had just been irritating. It had thrown the Magician's hat out of the window and mixed up all his socks. Then the Monster Maniac part began to overpower the Happy Birthday part. It had written very rude things about the Magician all over the walls and had thrown his supper into the fire.

But now the spell was getting dangerous; it wanted to get out. It coiled itself up like a huge spring and let out a roaring noise. The spell picked up the Magician and threw him at the window. The window flew open but the Magician, who was not exactly thin, got stuck.

The spell was furious. 'Get out, FAT ONE!' it screamed. It gave the Magician a wild push, he wobbled and began to fall. As he fell he managed to grab hold of the window-ledge.

The spell squeezed past him in a long, thin, wailing stream and rushed into the cold night air. Then it prised the Magician's fingers off the window-ledge and sent him tumbling down into the darkness.

The Magician fell away from the tower and before he could remember his Parachute Spell, he landed in the mud by the side of the moat – SPLAT!

He lay on his back and gazed up at the sky with a silly smile on his face.

'What lovely stars . . .' he murmured to himself. 'I wonder why I'm lying here in the mud?' The Magician could not remember anything much, but he had a strange idea that he ought to go and see Aunt Emilene. He staggered to his feet and started to totter over to the west wing.

Meanwhile, the spell had streamed off down the road to a small and nasty hut that was surrounded by huge signs. They said 'BEWARE OF THE MONSTER' and

'TRESPASSERS WILL BE PERSECUTED'.
Muriel would never go past the hut unless
Theobald was with her and they always ran
as fast as they could.

The spell banged on the door of the hut
and a tall, bony Thing answered it.

'You took your time,' the bony Thing complained.

'I am sooo sorry, Maaaster . . .' hissed the spell. 'I was mixed up with a revolting goody-goody spell. I have stamped on it now – *squish.*'

'Good. Where is he then, Godfrey, Magician of Crumbled Castle?' asked the Thing.

'I pushed him out, Master. But he got up. He goes towards the Emilene.'

'Aha – that's where I want him, right above my trap in the Emilene's kitchen. Take me there!'

The Thing clicked his long, bony fingers. The Monster Maniac Spell wound itself round the Thing and flew off with him to the west wing.

Far below them they saw the dazed Magician wandering along.

'It's him, the silly old baggins. He's not fit to live in a paper bag, let alone in my castle. Mine, mine, MINE!' shouted the Thing.

'Not yours yet, oh Master . . .' hissed the spell. 'OW!' The Thing dug its long nails into the black cloudy spell.

'Crumbled Castle will be mine by sunrise. But first, let's have some fun, HA, HA!' The Thing giggled and hurled a thunderflash just in front of the Magician.

CRACK! The Magician leapt into the air. Suddenly he remembered everything that had happened. He ran as fast as he could towards Aunt Emilene and the west wing.

CRACKLE! Another thunderflash landed beside him.

CRACKLE-CRACK! Yet another landed behind him as he dived into a large bush that grew below Aunt Emilene's kitchen window. Behind the bush was a small door. The Magician scrabbled in his pocket for the key and then very quietly put the key into the lock and turned it.

A moment later, a very muddy Magician scrambled out from underneath Aunt Emilene's sink.

 *Five*

'Godfrey!' exclaimed Aunt Emilene, who was carefully arranging her birthday cards on the kitchen table and wondering why he had not sent her one. 'What *are* you doing?'

The Magician left a trail of mud behind him as he stumbled over to the table and sat down.

'Cup of tea, please Ems?' he whispered.

'What? Go and get that mud off first–'

'Shhhh . . . it will hear you,' whispered the Magician.

'What will?' Aunt Emilene started whispering too.

Outside, the Thing chortled, 'I'll get you, Godfrey. It won't be long now!'

'That will . . .' whispered the Magician, looking very pale.

Aunt Emilene looked puzzled.

42

'You mean that's not Muriel playing one of her practical jokes?'

'Er, no. It's . . . um . . . a spell. I mixed up a Monster Maniac with a . . . well, I've made an awful mistake, Ems.'

Just then a thunderflash hit the kitchen wall.

Aunt Emilene jumped up. 'You haven't brought one *here* . . . I mean that isn't a Monster Maniac Spell outside?'

The Magician nodded, gabbling, 'Two pages stuck together . . . Muriel's jam sandwich . . .'

'You are just about the daftest brother possible, Godfrey. Where on earth did you pick up a nasty spell like that?' Aunt Emilene gasped as another thunderflash hit the wall and lit up the kitchen with a horrible red light.

'Er . . .' the Magician looked very sheepish. 'I . . . I got it from that peculiar Thing who lives in that awful old hut down the road. He sells really cheap spells.'

'You did WHAT?!' gasped Aunt Emilene, who knew a thing or two about spells.

'I *know* you said he was potty, but I thought he was quite interesting–'

'Stop wittering, Godfrey. Of course he was potty. Potty and nasty with it,' snapped

Aunt Emilene. 'The number of times I've found him slinking round the castle with his *Pocket Book of Bad Spells*. He's up to no good, I can tell you that.'

CRACK! This time a thunderflash hit the small door behind the bush.

'I'm coming to get you-HOO!' cackled the Thing. It threw another thunderflash at the door. The door shook and wobbled on its hinges.

Aunt Emilene grabbed hold of the Magician's hand. 'Quick, upstairs! We can hide in the secret cupboard in Muriel's bedroom.'

The Magician did not need telling twice. He rushed up the stairs behind Aunt Emilene. They ran all the way up to Muriel's room where there was an old bookcase full of her favourite stories. Aunt Emilene pulled out a copy of *Treasure Island* and the bookcase slid back to show a small cupboard where she and the Magician had often hidden when they were children. They scrambled in and the bookcase slid back again.

Then they sat and listened to the Monster Maniac Spell.

They heard it break down the door. They heard it rushing into the kitchen and throwing over the table. Then they heard it breaking Aunt Emilene's best china.

The Thing screamed, 'I'll find you . . . I know you're in here . . . I'm coming to get you-HOO . . . I'm coming to get you BOTH!'

'Happy Birthday, Ems,' whispered the Magician.

Aunt Emilene's reply was not as polite as it could have been.

Six

On the top of a wet and windy hill, a gust of wind blew Muriel along the road towards a dim blue light. It was the Borrible glowing gently in the dark. Behind the Borrible stood a very cold and damp elephant.

'Have you gone totally bananas, Theo?' yelled Muriel, who was just getting over the shock of being thrown off the bus and dumped on a dark and lonely road. 'What do you think you're doing, getting off a nice warm bus like that? Now we're stuck in the middle of nowhere and getting soaked – again.'

'WHAT?' yelled Theobald as a gust of wind blew his ears the wrong way.

The wind swirled round Muriel and almost blew her off her feet. She peered into the darkness trying to see where they were, then she grabbed hold of Theobald and

lifted him up above her head.

'MU, WHAT ARE YOU DOING NOW?' he protested.

'THEO, CAN YOU SEE ANYTHING?' yelled Muriel.

'PUT ME—'

CRACKLE-CRASH! A thunderflash lit up the hills in the distance and, suddenly, all three of them saw Crumbled Castle standing on the tallest hill, a dark shadow against the blue flashes.

'Wow . . .' breathed Muriel, still holding Theobald up above

48

her head.

'PUT ME DOWN MU!' he yelled. Muriel put him down.

'What's going on there, Theo? That's more than just a storm.'

Another thunderflash lit up the castle.

'I don't like the look of that, Mu,' said Theobald. 'Come on, let's get going. At least we know where we are now.'

They started off down the hill with the Borrible trotting after them.

At the bottom of the hill they came to the edge of a wood. It looked dark, cold and unfriendly. The wind rustled the branches and Muriel was sure she could see things moving between the trees. She stopped and shivered.

'It's all right, Mu,' said Theobald.

The Borrible pushed forwards. 'I'll go first,' it said in a low rumbly voice.

'It talks!' squeaked Muriel in surprise.

'Don't be rude, Mu.' whispered

Theobald. 'Of course it talks. Borribles do talk.'

'Well how was I to know that?'

'Didn't the Magician ever tell you about Boris? He could talk *and* hum tunes,' said Theobald.

The Borrible plunged into the wood and Theobald pulled Muriel along behind him. They trod carefully through the dark dripping wood, following the pale blue light of the Borrible. It began to hum quietly to itself: 'Hum-de-hum-de-hum-de-hum . . .' over and over again.

Not so far away, in Aunt Emilene's sitting-room, the Thing stopped pulling feathers out of the cushions and listened to the far-off sound of humming.

'Nooo . . .' it hissed to itself. 'Not YOU . . . you horrible Borrible.'

It grabbed hold of the spell with its bony fingers. 'Take me outside,' it hissed.

The spell streamed up the chimney and

settled on to the roof. The Thing squatted beside it and listened hard. In the distance it heard a horribly familiar sound coming from the wood at the bottom of the hill, 'Hum-du-hum-de-hum-de-hum . . .'

'It is the Borrible,' hissed the Thing. 'We

must frighten it away before it gets to the spellbook.' It put its hands over its ears, 'Aaargh, that humming goes round and round inside my head!

Down in the dark wood the humming was going round and round inside Muriel's head too.

'What *is* that tune, Theo?' she whispered. 'Sounds familiar.'

'Don't know Mu. I'm sure I've heard it before too. Hum-de-hum–'

'Do shut up, Theo, it's bad enough with him humming it,' snapped Muriel, who was feeling very tired by now and still scared. She had a strange feeling that something was watching them.

Muriel was right, something *was* watching them. A Monster Maniac Spell crouched just above them. It carefully watched them as they followed the blue light of the Borrible through the wood towards Crumbled Castle.

Theobald was still humming the tune.

'It's "Humpty Dumpty", Mu!' he said. Muriel felt cross and jumpy.

'I think your brain stuffing must have got wet, Theo,' she snapped.

Theobald was about to comment on Muriel's complete lack of brain stuffing when the Monster Maniac Spell hurled itself at them. With a horrible scream the Thing ran out after the spell and clawed at the Borrible. The Borrible stamped on its thin, bony foot.

'OW-EE!' yelled the Thing and kicked the Borrible. Then the Monster Maniac Spell gathered up the Thing and together they hurled themselves, screaming and howling at the Borrible. Muriel and Theobald were caught up in the smelly black cloud of the Spell, Muriel grabbed on to the Borrible as the Thing screamed, 'GO AWAY GO AWAY GO AWAY!'

The Borrible roared the loudest, fiercest roar that Muriel had ever heard. The spell and the Thing took off in fright, up through the trees and back to Crumbled Castle.

The wood was left strangely quiet and still.

'Are you all right, Theo?' whispered Muriel.

There was no reply.

'Theo . . . Theo . . .? THEO, WHERE ARE YOU?'

Theobald had disappeared.

'Theo – Theo's GONE!' cried Muriel. 'It's taken Theo! THEO, THEO, COME BACK!'

Seven

'THEO, THEO!' yelled Muriel. She tore through the wood, leaping over dead branches and dodging round the trees. The Borrible thumped along behind her.

Suddenly they were out of the wood, standing breathless at the bottom of the steep hill that led up to Crumbled Castle.

The castle was strangely quiet, but not in a peaceful way. It was quiet in a watchful, waiting way. Muriel and the Borrible climbed up the damp, slippery grass of the hill and made their way through the broken main gate. It was very dark but Muriel could see just enough by the blue light of the Borrible.

They stopped in the courtyard at the bottom of the Magician's tower. Muriel looked up hoping to see a light at the window but there was nothing there.

'Where is he, what's happened?' whispered Muriel, wondering if she ought to go up and see if the Magician was there.

She did not notice the Borrible squeeze itself through the entrance to the tower and start climbing the stairs up to the Magician's room.

Suddenly Muriel was alone.

'Aaaargh!' yelled Muriel. The sound

echoed round the empty castle courtyard. Muriel had had enough. She ran. She was going home to Auntie Ems in the west wing and nothing was going to stop her.

Sitting in Aunt Emilene's kitchen was the Thing, with the Monster Maniac Spell curled up at its feet. It sat quietly holding on to Theobald by his trunk. It was trying to decide whether to give him to the Monster Maniac Spell to throw off the roof or to keep him.

'I will keep it, it may come in useful.' The Thing threw Theobald into Aunt Emilene's oven and closed the door.

'Stay there, elephant. Don't go away, HA HA. Now for the little Muriel. And did I hear a little Muriel-sound from the courtyard only a moment ago? Oh, I think I did.' The Thing giggled. It wrapped the Monster Maniac Spell around itself and flew off to find Muriel.

A moment later, Muriel reached the end of the last dark corridor that joined the castle courtyard to the west wing. She grabbed the handle of the heavy wooden door that led into the kitchen and pushed hard. The door was locked.

Muriel banged frantically on the door. 'Auntie Ems, Auntie Ems! Let me in, let me in!'

Up at the top of the west wing, behind the bookcase in Muriel's bedroom, Aunt Emilene heard the banging and shouting.

'It's Muriel,' she whispered to the Magician.

She pushed the bookcase to one side and was about to rush out of their hiding-place when the Magician grabbed hold of her jumper and dragged her back.

'Emilene, that's the Monster Maniac Spell! It's sounding like Muriel to make us come out. You can't go down there.'

'It's Muriel, I'm sure it is Muriel. We can't leave her out there with that Monster Maniac Spell about, Godfrey,' said Aunt Emilene.

'No Emilene, it's not Muriel. Come back!' The Magician dived after Aunt Emilene and tripped over one of Muriel's teddies. 'Ouch!'

Aunt Emilene ignored him. She marched out of Muriel's bedroom and bravely went down to the kitchen.

The Magician followed her.

'Emilene,' he said, tiptoeing carefully down the stairs at a safe distance behind her. 'Be reasonable.

We're both worried about Muriel but it won't help her if we let the Monster Maniac Spell get us, will it?'

'And it certainly won't help Muriel if we let the Monster Maniac Spell get *her*, will it?' said Aunt Emilene as she reached the kitchen. She peered in and breathed a sigh of relief.

'Well Godfrey, you'll be pleased to know your Monster Maniac Spell has gone out for a little bit of fresh air.'

'AUNTIE EMS!!!' Muriel pushed desperately at the door.

Aunt Emilene pulled the door open and Muriel fell into the kitchen.

'Th-Th-THEO!' wailed Muriel.

There was a small sound from Aunt Emilene's oven but nobody noticed it.

'Shhhh, dear,' cooed Aunt Emilene soothingly. 'You're safe now.' She gathered Muriel up and wrapped her in an old flowery tablecloth that she had pulled out from under a pile of knives and forks.

'You're soaked,' tutted Aunt Emilene. 'What have you been doing out this late? Godfrey, what were you thinking of, letting Muriel go out and about at night with a Monster Maniac Spell on the loose?'

'Theo's gone . . .' stammered Muriel.

'There, there. Shhh now,' said Aunt Emilene soothingly.

The Magician was hopping up and down anxiously. 'Have you got the shopping, Muriel?' he asked.

Aunt Emilene looked exasperated; 'Shopping? *Shopping*? At a time like this? Sometimes I wonder about you, Godfrey.'

Muriel tried again: 'But Theo's–'

'Where's the shopping, Muriel?' the Magician repeated. For some reason he was having trouble keeping his balance and he slid across the floor. Muriel wished he would keep still.

'If you would just let me have the

61

shopping then I could–'

'GODFREY!' exploded Great Aunt Emilene. She kicked away a saucepan that was rolling towards her. 'Do stop blethering on about your wretched shopping.'

'Auntie Ems. Theo, he's been–'

Something rattled inside Aunt Emilene's oven. The Magician went very pale. 'The spell's back!' he whispered. 'Muriel, I MUST HAVE THE SHOPPING!'

'I didn't get the shopping, I–' Muriel began to feel a little seasick. It felt as though the floor was moving. She watched the Magician slide past her again into an upturned cactus.

'OUCH! You didn't get it? What do you mean you DIDN'T GET IT?' The Magician looked horrified.

'She means she didn't get it, Godfrey. You should do your own shopping. Muriel has more important things to do than go out buying your chocolate biscuits or whatever,' snapped Aunt Emilene who was now sliding gracefully towards the Magician and the cactus.

'THEO'S GONE!' exclaimed Muriel. 'Why don't you listen to me?'

But nobody was listening, they were too busy trying to work out what was happening to the kitchen. A large dip had appeared in the middle of the kitchen floor and everything, including Aunt Emilene and the Magician, was sliding towards it. Muriel hung on tightly to the oven which was about the only thing that wasn't making its way to the middle of the kitchen.

'Did you say something, Muriel dear?' asked Aunt Emilene as she tried to get out of the way of a bucket.

Muriel took a deep breath and wailed, 'THEO'S BEEN KIDNAPPED BY A HORRIBLE SMELLY BLACK CLOUD. HE'S GONE!'

'Excuse me, I'm in here,' said a small voice from inside the oven. 'Could you open the door please?'

Eight

Muriel sat by the oven, cuddling Theo.

'Give over, Mu,' spluttered Theo from underneath a damp flowery tablecloth.

'Theo, how did you get in there?' Muriel asked happily. 'I thought you'd been . . . well I didn't think you were hiding in Auntie Em's oven.'

'I wasn't *hiding* there, Mu. Something put me in there–' Theobald caught sight of

Aunt Emilene and the Magician who were standing in 'a hole, which had just appeared in the middle of the kitchen floor, and looking very confused.

'Mu, what are they doing in there?' he whispered.

'Oh, crumbs, Theo, I don't know. I was so pleased you were all right that I didn't notice them. Auntie Ems, can you get out?'

'No, I don't think so, dear. It's a bit deep.'

The kitchen gave a sudden shake. A thunderflash hit the little door under the sink and it flew open. Aunt Emilene stared out from the edge of the hole. 'Oh no,' she whispered, 'it's coming back.'

Crawling out from underneath the sink came the Thing, closely followed by the seeping black cloud of the Monster Maniac Spell.

'I knew it!' gasped Aunt Emilene. 'Look Godfrey, it's him, the one you bought the spell from. It's that horrible Thing from down the road!'

'Tut, tut. Mind your manners now, Emilene,' hissed the Thing. 'Not that you'll need them where you're going.'

The Thing looked at the hole in the kitchen floor. It smiled a menacing smile, showing its broken yellow teeth. 'Lovely, my trap is working nicely. You'll both be on your way down soon, HA HA!'

It settled down beside the Magician and put its bony arm round him. It hissed into his ear, spraying spit down his neck. 'I like your little castle, Godfrey, and your

cutesy little tower where you do all your pathetic tricks. You know, I've always liked it, Godfrey.'

The Magician shivered and slipped down a bit further. The Thing giggled. 'I knew you were a cheapskate magician, Godfrey. I knew that one day you would come into my little hut and buy one of my spells for your spellbook if it was cheap enough. Then all I had to do was get you to use it and my powers would be released. Crumbled Castle would be mine, HA HA! Who do you think squashed that disgusting little jam sandwich into your spellbook? You never even noticed me, did you Godfrey?'

Aunt Emilene was cross. '*I* noticed you, you horrible sneak. I noticed you creeping round the castle, breaking things and throwing them about, trying to get rid of us. Don't think I don't know who threw that washbasin at me.'

68

'Be quiet, oh windbag one!' the Thing hissed. 'Oh, but soon you *will* be quiet. So very, very quiet. You and this so-called Magician will be locked forever in my deepest, darkest cavern underneath the Dark Mountain. See, the ground is opening up far beneath you, ready for you both to drop down, down, DOWN!'

The kitchen floor shuddered and Aunt Emilene and the Magician began to disappear. They grabbed hold of the edge and all Muriel could see were four hands hanging on to the slippery lino.

'You horrible Thing,' yelled Muriel. 'You let my Auntie Ems go!'

'Muriel, what about me?' the Magician's quavering voice wafted out of the hole.

'Oh, and the Magician too. You let them both go!'

'Oh, what a talkative little Muriel,' hissed the Thing. 'I like your student, Godfrey. I will have that, it will be mine, HA

HA! I will have its elephant too; it will be useful to do the cooking. Oh come here, little studenty thing . . .'

The Monster Maniac Spell uncurled itself and wafted over to Muriel and Theobald. It began to wrap itself round them, tighter and tighter.

'Heeelp . . .' spluttered Muriel. But no one could help.

Aunt Emilene and the Magician could do nothing, they were hanging on to the edge of a very deep, dark hole. Far below them they could hear a shrill whistling, it was the sound of the freezing winds that blew through the caverns underneath the Dark Mountain.

Nine

The Monster Maniac Spell curled itself round Muriel and Theobald like a huge black snake. Aunt Emilene stared in horror.

'Oh no, Godfrey, look . . .'she whispered.

The Magician looked, but he didn't look at Muriel and Theobald. He looked down instead.

'Aaaargh!' he yelled and let go of the edge. As he fell he grabbed on to Aunt Emilene's feet and hung there, swaying above the three-kilometre drop. Aunt Emilene's hands began to slip with the extra weight of the Magician.

The Thing did a little dance round the kitchen and cackled, 'Oh what fun, I have waited so long to see this. At last it will be me who is the Magician here. Not a soppy Magician like you, Godfrey, but a powerful Magician of the Darkness. I shall remember this day for a long time, oh yes . . . oh–'

Suddenly the Thing stopped laughing and stood very still.

'YOU . . . with the spellbook . . .'

The Thing was staring at the doorway into the kitchen. A humming sound floated through the door, 'Hum-de-hum-de-hum-de-hum . . .'

'"Humpty Dumpty"!' shouted Aunt Emilene.

'Don't be silly, Emilene,' came the voice of the Magician. 'This is no time for jokes.'

The Borrible walked into the kitchen, casting a flickering blue light over everything. He was clutching the Magician's spellbook closely to him and happily humming 'Humpty Dumpty'.

'Hello, Emilene,' he said. 'Got a bit of trouble here?'

'What's that?' came the Magician's voice from somewhere below the kitchen floor.

'It's Boris, Godfrey. BORIS!'

I don't think that's very funny, Emilene. Not at a time like this.'

The Borrible peered over the edge of the hole. 'Hello, Godfrey. Long time, no see.'

'Aaargh!' yelled the Magician and let go of Aunt Emilene's feet. He tumbled down, down into the three-kilometre drop towards the deepest, darkest cavern below the Dark Mountain. Faster and faster he fell until he remembered the words of the Parachute Spell. Then he wafted gently down through the cold dark air which got colder and darker, darker and colder as he slowly but surely fell towards the cavern.

The Borrible pushed the Thing aside and pulled Aunt Emilene out of the hole. She grabbed hold of him and pointed towards the Monster Maniac Spell which was trying to sneak Muriel and Theobald out of the door without being noticed.

'Boris, listen; it's got Muriel and Theobald. It's a cheap Monster Maniac Spell which Godfrey bought from that nasty Thing. It's taken over a Happy Birthday Spell. Been going for at least two days.'

The Thing shrank back. It knew that it was in *bad* trouble. Boris Borrible on his own was a nuisance but Boris Borrible with the spellbook was unbeatable. 'Go away,' it quavered.

Boris Borrible did not go away. He was busy looking in the spellbook. He peeled off a squashed jam sandwich and unstuck the pages.

The Thing sidled up to the Borrible. 'I am sooo sorry,' it whispered. 'So sorry that I locked you in that chest all those years ago. So sorry that I dried you out and sold you to the Magic Shop. I had to get rid of you – you made that idiot Godfrey too powerful. You were too good for him, Boris. I knew that if you went he'd make a mistake one day. I had to do it. You do understand that, don't you? I'm sure we could come to some . . . arrangement. I shall be the most powerful in the land, you could be my helper–'

'No!' boomed Boris. He slammed the spellbook shut with a bang. Then he started humming 'Happy Birthday'. Slowly the Happy Birthday Spell began to take over from the Monster Maniac Spell. The black cloud around Muriel and Theobald unwound itself and disappeared. Muriel and Theobald landed with a bump on the floor.

They watched Boris Borrible walk over

to the Thing. The Thing huddled in a corner and tried to hide under a tea-towel. Aunt Emilene jumped up and snatched the tea-towel back.

'Oh no you don't. I've just washed that.' Boris Borrible held up the spellbook and started reading from it in a loud rumbly voice. Muriel peered over to see what he was reading from, it was the Say Goodbye To Pests and Fleas, A Hygenic Castle in Only Twenty Seconds Spell. With Boris Borrible doing the spell, the Thing had as much chance as the average castle cockroach.

Twenty seconds later, the Thing had shrivelled up into nothing. All that was left was a crumpled black jumpsuit.

The Borrible carefully picked it up, holding it at arm's length. He whirled the jumpsuit round his head and threw it out of the window. Muriel, Theobald and Aunt Emilene watched as it flapped about helplessly, then the wind took it and blew it away up into the mountains.

They never saw it again, but a few days later two mountain goats ate a rather unusual supper and did not sleep very well that night.

Ten

'So if Theo and I had sung Happy Birthday, the Monster Maniac Spell would have gone?' Muriel asked the Borrible.

'Maybe . . .' said Boris sleepily. He settled himself down on a couple of cushions and yawned. 'You could have used some Twin Stars, Still Dust and Truth Paste . . . none of those in the store cupboard though . . . It's been a long day . . . Tell Godfrey to wake me up for breakfast.' With that the Borrible started snoring.

'*Godfrey*! Oh my goodness me, I quite forgot,' squeaked Aunt Emilene, 'He fell down the hole!'

Muriel, Theobald and Aunt Emilene peered into the gaping hole in the middle of the kitchen. It was pitch black and very cold. There was no sign of the Magician.

'He's gone,' sniffed Muriel. 'It's all my fault. Now I know why he wanted those Twin Stars, Still Dust and Truth Paste. If I had got his shopping in the Magic Shop then none of this would have happened.'

'Don't be daft, Mu,' said Theobald. 'It was his fault, he should never have bought that Monster Maniac Spell from the Thing. Anyway, you got Boris back. I thought it was just any old Borrible, but you found Boris, Mu – after all those years!'

The sound of snoring drifted across the kitchen. 'Well, he's not much use now, is he?' said Muriel

'You mean Muriel got Boris back?' asked Aunt Emilene.

'Yes, she did,' said Theobald proudly.

'Did I?' said Muriel, surprised to have done something right at last. 'Well, perhaps I could get the Magician back too,' she said. She went over to the snoring Borrible and picked up the Magician's spellbook which lay beside him.

Muriel turned over the pages of the spellbook. It was exciting, she had never been allowed to look in it before.

'Mu, you shouldn't really look in there,' muttered Theobald.

'I've got to, Theo. Anyway, it doesn't look that difficult to me. I don't see what he makes all the fuss about.'

Muriel looked up three spells: the Parachute Spell, the Dark and Gloomy Places Rescue Spell and How To Be a Tower-block Lift Spell.

'That should do it,' she muttered and scribbled down the spells on her hand so that she would remember them.

Theobald looked worried. 'I don't think you should go on your own, Mu,' he said; 'I'll come with you.'

'I'll come too, Muriel,' said Aunt Emilene. 'You don't know nearly enough about spells to go off to some nasty cavern full of . . . well, who knows what that Thing keeps down there.'

'We can't all go, Auntie Ems,' said Muriel, digging a torch out from under an upturned drawer. 'They'll only work for one person. Anyway, it was my idea and I want to do it.'

'No Mu, DON'T!' said Theobald.

'Back soon, Theo.' With that Muriel jumped off the side of the hole and dropped down into the darkness. It was very cold, much colder than she had expected and the air made a loud roaring noise as it rushed past her ears.

Tumbling down the hole, Muriel said

to herself, 'Oh, what have I done?' Then she said, 'Turn the torch on and stop being silly, Muriel.'

She turned the torch on and looked at her hand. She found the Parachute Spell. Muriel said the Parachute Spell and, much to her relief, she slowed down. The air stopped rushing past and everything became very quiet. As she floated down, Muriel tried to learn the the Dark and Gloomy Places Rescue Spell.

Soon Muriel was in a very dark and gloomy place. The Parachute Spell had dropped her gently on the floor of the cavern, and at once the freezing air numbed her fingers and froze her nose. It was so cold that Muriel could hardly breathe and her hand shook as she shone her torch round, looking for the Magician.

'Go away . . . er . . . please . . .' came the Magician's trembly voice from behind a rock. 'Um . . . I am a very big and fierce monster . . . Grrrr.'

Muriel would have giggled if the cavern had not been quite so cold and scary. She said the the Dark and Gloomy Places Rescue Spell and the Magician whooshed out from behind the rock and found himself standing next to Muriel.

'Oh . . . M-M-Muriel,' his teeth chattered.

'Has that Th-Th-Thing got you too?'

'N-no,' said Muriel, jumping up and

down trying to stop her toes from freezing. 'I have c-c-come to rescue you.'

Muriel had been looking forward to saying that all the way down and she could not help smiling, even if she was colder than the average fishfinger straight from the freezer. She did not notice a dark shape oozing out from behind one of the rocks and creeping up behind them. Claw-like shadows reached out towards Muriel and the Magician.

BANG-FIZZ! The Dark and Gloomy Places Rescue Spell sprang into action. It swatted away the oozing shadows and whisked Muriel and the Magician up and away. Muriel remembered the How To be a Tower-block Lift Spell and in no time at all she and the Magician were rushing upwards towards the surface. They stopped a couple of times for no particular reason before they shot out into the kitchen and landed on top of an amazed Aunt Emilene and Theobald.

Eleven

'Er . . . thank you, Muriel,' mumbled the Magician in an embarrassed voice. He picked himself up from the top of the heap of three people and one elephant piled on the kitchen floor.

'S'all right, it was easy really,' said Muriel happily as she pulled Theobald out from under Aunt Emilene's foot.

'Thanks, Mu. Phew that's better.'

Aunt Emilene staggered to her feet and looked at the mess strewn round her kitchen. She stared at the hole in her kitchen floor and said grumpily, 'Can you manage to fill that in, Godfrey? I don't want to be falling three kilometres down every time I go to do the washing-up. On second thoughts, perhaps I'd better wait until Boris wakes up before you try another spell.

Or shall I ask your Grade Two student to fill it in?'

'Muriel is only Grade One,' sniffed the Magician, 'and a repeat year at that. She's been bunking off classes all year *and* she forgot the shopping. I don't suppose she did her homework either.'

'And who's fault was it that you needed the shopping in the first place?' Aunt Emilene picked up one of her favourite china ducks from the floor. Its head had broken off.

'That is not the point,' said the Magician huffily.

'And as for the homework, Godfrey, perhaps you'd like to take a look over there.'

Aunt Emilene pointed to Boris Borrible who was fast asleep in the corner.

'Oh my, it really is Boris Borrible.' The Magician tiptoed over to the Borrible. He gently poked him. 'He is real after all. I can hardly believe it.' The Magician sat down next to Boris and put his arm round him. The Borrible snuffled in his sleep, turned over and started snoring again.

'What's my Boris coming back got to do

with Muriel?' the Magician asked suspiciously.

'Boris was my homework,' said Muriel.

'You mean you went and found Boris for me? Well, I don't know what to say . . .'

'You could say that I'm Grade Two now,' said Muriel, who was amazed at how well everything was working out for a change.

'Oh . . . all right then.' The Magician was still staring at Boris Borrible. 'As long as you do your homework from now on. And I'll have my spellbook back, thank you.' The Magician picked up his spellbook but Aunt Emilene snatched it from him.

'Oh no you don't, Godfrey. You wait until Boris wakes up before you try any more spells.' She very busily started sweeping up her smashed plates.

'I'll only do half a spell, Emilene,' said the Magician.

Aunt Emilene did not hear him, she was noisily emptying her plates into the bin.

'It's the other half of the Happy Birthday Spell,' whispered the Magician to Muriel. 'She won't mind.'

There was a big puff of pink smoke and a loud POP!

'Aaargh!' screamed Aunt Emilene.

CRASH! she dropped the only plate that had not been broken. She swung round and was about to yell something very rude at the Magician when a big, slightly squashed, pink birthday cake appeared with four balloons and a large present.

'Happy Birthday!' said Muriel, Theobald and the Magician.

'Well, I don't know what to say. Thank you Godfrey.' Aunt Emilene laughed, 'And a spell that worked, too!'

'Er . . . I don't know where the streamers have got to,' mumbled the Magician looking round.

'Here they are,' said Muriel. She reached up into the pink smoke and pulled out a

cascade of coloured streamers and threw
them over Aunt Emilene.

'Happy Birthday, Auntie Ems!'

Other Story Books also published by
Hodder Children's Books

61954 6	Hamish	£2.99	☐
	W. J. Corbett		
63462 6	A Game of Catch	£2.99	☐
63461 8	The Little Sea Horse	£2.99	☐
	Helen Cresswell		
63596 7	The Spooks of Biddlecombe Manor	£2.99	☐
64837 6	Spooks to the Rescue	£2.99	☐
	Andrew Matthews		
64846 5	Muriel and the Mystery Tour	£2.99	☐
	Angie Sage		
62653 4	Prince Vince and the Case of the Smelly Goat	£2.99	☐
62654 2	Prince Vince and Hot Diggory Dog	£2.99	☐
	Valerie Wilding		

All Hodder Children's books are available at your local bookshop or newsagent, or can be ordered direct from the publisher. Just tick the the titles you want and fill in the form below. Prices and availability subject to change without notice.

Hodder Children's Books, Cash Sales Department, Bookpoint, 39 Milton Park, Abingdon, OXON, OX14 4TD, UK. If you have a credit card you may order by telephone – 01235 831700.

Please enclose a cheque or postal order made payable to Bookpoint Ltd to the value of the cover price and allow the following for postage and packing:

UK & BFPO – £1.00 for the first book, 50p for the second book, and 30p for each additional book ordered up to a maximum charge of £3.00.

OVERSEAS & EIRE – £2.00 for the first book, £1.00 for the second book, and 50p for each additional book.

Name

Address

If you would prefer to pay by credit card, please complete:
Please debit my VISA/Access/Diner's Card/ American Express (delete as applicable) card number:

Signature

Expiry date
